MARVEL
SUPER HERO
ADVENTURES

Deck the Malls!

With Spider-Man, Spider-Gwen, and Venom

By **Mackenzie Cadenhead**
& Sean Ryan

Illustrated by **Derek Laufman**

MARVEL
Los Angeles
New York

Dedication
For Phinn and Lyra —MC
For Mom and Dad —SR

marvelkids.com

Designed by David Roe

Printed in the United States of America
First Paperback Edition, September 2017
10 9 8 7 6 5 4 3 2 1
Library of Congress Control Number: 2017931520
ISBN 978-1-368-00579-1
FAC-029261-17202

Spider-Man

Peter Parker was just a normal kid when he was bitten by a radioactive spider and became **The Amazing Spider-Man**! He has super strength, can climb walls, and can jump incredible distances. Being the science-minded kid that he is, Peter also made his very own web-shooters. Peter takes his job as a Super Hero seriously because of the lesson his Uncle Ben taught him: With great power comes great responsibility.

Spider-Gwen

Gwen Stacy isn't just Peter Parker's friend and the drummer in a totally awesome rock band. She's also got the same spider powers as our favorite web-slinger and fights crime as **Spider-Gwen!** Gwen is the daughter of Police Captain George Stacy. Guess you could say that taking down criminals is in her blood!

Venom

Venom is an alien creature that can only take form by attaching itself to a person's body. It takes control of that person's movements and mind—just like you do with a puppet but way creepier! These days Venom is attached to a guy named Eddie Brock. But Eddie's just a regular dude, and Venom wants more skill, more strength, more everything! What better host to get all this from than your friendly neighborhood Spider-Man?! If it can attach itself to the wall-crawler, Venom will have more power than it's ever known!

Chapter 1

"Thirty-five, thirty-six, thirty-seven," Peter Parker said. He counted down each person standing in the line outside Easy Ernie's Electronics, a store inside the Forest Hills Mall. The line was long. Peter and his Aunt May stood at the back of it. Peter gasped. "There are thirty-seven people ahead of us!"

Aunt May laid her hand on her nephew's shoulder. "Why don't we come back later?" she suggested. "Perhaps the line will be shorter."

Peter's mouth dropped open. "Come

back later?!" he whined. "But the new Stark Enterprises Smart Watch could be sold out by then!"

"Peter, we have so much holiday shopping to do today," Aunt May explained. "We can't spend all of our time in line at one store."

Peter stomped his foot. He crossed his arms. His eyebrows pulled together, and his mouth puckered into a pout. May Parker had not seen her nephew throw a tantrum in many years. She tried hard not to laugh.

"Aunt May," Peter said. "The Stark Smart Watch is the most exciting advance in personal computing technology since the Stark Pad. This watch will change my life!"

Aunt May asked, "How?"

Peter blinked. He looked to the ceiling. Then he looked at his feet. "Um . . . I don't know exactly how yet. But I'm sure it will! Please, please, please? It's all I want for Christmas!"

Aunt May did not understand technological gadgets. What she *did* know was that Peter was a good kid. He had been all year long. If she could do something to make him this happy, it was hard for her to say no. She smiled and said, "Who am I to question a watch's life-changing abilities? All right, Peter. I will get you the watch as your gift this year."

Peter clapped his hands. "Thank you, thank you!" he said. He gave his aunt a hug. Then he slung his backpack over his shoulder and began to walk away.

"Peter," Aunt May said. "Where are you going?"

"I have a lot of shopping to do," he replied. "I can't spend the whole day waiting in line for my own present! I will stop by when I'm done to see how far you've gotten." As he walked off, he waved. "Thanks again. You're the best!"

Aunt May watched her nephew disappear into the holiday-shopping crowd. Though Peter often ran off for reasons unknown to her, at least today she knew where he was and what he was doing.

She looked at her shopping list. She sighed.

"Candy cane?" asked the gentleman in line behind her.

Aunt May took the treat. "Don't mind if I do."

Chapter
2

"This would look good with my new smart watch," Peter said to himself. He held up a navy blue sweater with brown patches at the elbows. He looked in the mirror. "Sharp," he told his reflection. "Let's add it to the wish list."

When Peter left Aunt May waiting in line at Easy Ernie's, his plan was to buy holiday presents for his friends and family. But as he walked through the mall he saw a lot of things he wanted for himself! Sure, the holidays were about giving. But if people wanted to give to him, shouldn't he have a few suggestions ready?

Peter entered a bookstore. He wanted to get the latest Agatha Twisty mystery as a present for Aunt May. However, as he passed the science section, he stopped. It wouldn't hurt to check out the new releases, right?

Ten minutes later he was still leafing through the books and grinning like an elf in Santa's workshop. "Oh boy!" he said to himself. "These definitely need to go on my wish list too!"

Peter usually didn't think only of himself. In fact, most of the time Peter thought about everyone else. Because Peter Parker was Spider-Man, the wall-crawling, web-slinging Super Hero. For him, helping others was the name of the game. Peter lived his life by the lesson that his late Uncle Ben taught him: With great power comes great responsibility. But every now and then—usually when presents were involved—Peter Parker the "me-me-me kid" took over. Today was that day.

Peter imagined a stack of new science books in gingerbread-man wrapping paper. Then a girl's voice interrupted his daydream.

"Hey, Pete," the girl said. She gave him a hug. "What are you up to?"

"Oh, hi, Gwen," said Peter. His imaginary tower of presents toppled to the ground. "Holiday shopping. You?"

"Same thing," Gwen Stacy replied. "I have so many people to shop for. And I don't know what to get my dad. What

do you get the police captain who has everything?"

"Uh-huh," Peter said. In his mind he placed the wrapped science books beside a gift bag containing the sweater.

"Maybe you can help!" Gwen suggested. "Dad likes to run. Let's see if there's something good in the sports section."

Gwen Stacy was smart. She was funny. She was kind. Peter liked hanging out with her, a lot. Normally, helping her find a present for her father would be fun. But today, Peter had other things to do.

"Sorry, Gwen," he said. "I can't."

Gwen looked surprised. "Come on, Pete. I could really use your help. It will only take a minute."

Peter thought of the toy store he

wanted to visit before lunch and of the remote-controlled drone he wanted to play with. "Don't have a minute to spare," he said. He was already walking away. Halfway to the exit he shouted, "See you around!"

"See you around," Gwen replied. But Peter was too far gone to hear.

Chapter 3

Gwen stood alone in the bookstore. She thought, Well, that was rude!

Gwen Stacy knew Peter better than most people did. She knew he was generous. She knew he was helpful. She even knew he was Spider-Man!* The Peter who didn't have time to help his friend was not the Peter she knew.

Gwen did not like this one bit.

There were many people in Gwen's life on whom she could rely. She was the drummer in a totally awesome

---

Told you she knew him really well!

all-girl rock band called the Mary Janes, and her bandmates were like sisters. Her dad was the coolest. And she could always rely on herself.

But Gwen's relationship with Peter was special. Not only did she know his secret, but he also knew hers.

Gwen had been bitten by a radioactive spider just like the one that bit Peter. Like Peter, she also developed super powers. Wall-climbing? Check. Super strength? Of course. Web-shooters? Do you even need to ask? With these powers, Gwen began to fight crime. She and Spider-Man even teamed up from time to time.

And okay, sometimes Peter could be a little bit of a know-it-all. Just because he had been a Spider-Person longer than she had didn't mean he knew everything! But to walk away like that? To be so focused on himself? To *not* help? No, this was not the Peter Parker *or* Spider-Man Gwen knew.

And Gwen was going to tell him so. Right after she bought her father a copy of *Running Fast with Fartleks.***

***Why are you laughing? A fartlek is just the name of an exercise for people who like to run. It's just a fartlek. Stop laughing! Get your mind out of the bathroom!*

Chapter 4

Peter walked through the mall. Twinkling lights framed snowy window displays. Wreaths and garlands decorated the food court. A Christmas tree stood tall beside a menorah and a kinara. Families gathered around a group of carolers singing "Deck the Halls."

"I love the holidays," Peter said. "Everyone is in such a festive mood, they don't even care that I'm talking to myself!"

Peter bounced down the hallway.

All that stood between him and the toy store were the carolers, a department store, the food court, Santa's workshop, and the alien creature that had been following him for the last ten minutes.

That creature's name was Venom. And it wanted Peter like a kid wants a snow day. On its own, the creature was just a pile of sticky, black goo—worse than anything you've ever found on the bottom of your shoe. But when it attached itself to a person, it could take their shape and control them—

like a clinging wet bathing suit, if that bathing suit could make you do stuff and was a really bad dude.

Though Venom was currently attached to a man named Eddie, it was Peter that the alien wanted.

"We must attach ourself to the strongest, fastest, most powerful human," Venom hissed. "We know that Peter Parker is Spider-Man. If

we control his spider powers, we control the world! We must have him!"

Venom perched on a rafter. Peter neared the carolers. Just as the alien was about to jump, the singers began to sing "Jingle Bells." Their voices were as loud as the jangling sleigh bells they shook.

Venom shivered. The black goo vibrated. It began to separate from Eddie. It ran away from the noise. In the quiet, it pulled itself back together.

"We hate the holidays," Venom said. "So much loudness. Carolers, bells, people laughing! Humbug! We will wait for Peter Parker to get to a less noisy place. Then we will attack!"

As soon as Peter was in a quieter spot, that's exactly what Venom did.

"Oof!" said Peter.

"Hiss!" said Venom.

The alien creature pounced on the teenager, sending him flying into the department store.

Peter got to his feet. Venom charged toward him. Peter ran away.

"Changing room, changing room, changing room," Peter chanted. He raced through the accessories section in search of a private place to become Spider-Man. He couldn't be seen fighting foes as Peter Parker. He needed his Super Hero identity. He had to slow Venom down. He had to do it now!

Peter grabbed whatever he could and tossed it at the alien. A scarf. A handful of fake snow. A top hat. The items hit Venom hard. Venom caught sight of itself in the mirror and hissed.

"We look like Frosty the Snowman!" the alien screeched. "We will get you for this!" Venom looked around. Peter was nowhere to be seen. "Come out, come out, wherever you are. You cannot hide from us! Show yourself, Spider—"

Wham!

Spider-Man burst out of a changing room feet first. He knocked the wind

out of—and the clothing off of—Venom.

"Man," Spidey said. "You were going to say 'man,' right?"

Venom retreated to the food court. Spider-Man followed.

The alien and the wall-crawler faced off at the center of a holiday-centric fast-food fantasy. Spider-Man slammed Venom into a display of snowman snow cones. Venom threw Spidey into a Christmas tree pizza.

"I get it," Spider-Man said. "The ornaments are pepperoni. Cute!"

The Super Hero and the Super Villain grappled through reindeer rugelach, candy cane calzones, and eggnog egg rolls. When Venom finally tossed Spidey into a tower of latke tacos, the web-slinger was out of food and out of ideas.

"Oy vey," Spider-Man said. "I could really use some help."

Chapter 6

"That was the third time I saw Ms. Marvel in person, but only the second time in New Jersey." The man who had given Aunt May a candy cane was scrolling through photos on his Stark Phone Six. "Here's the fourth time I saw her. I'm pretty sure she recognized me. See? She looks like she's smiling!"

The line at Easy Ernie's had moved less than five feet since Peter left. Aunt May knew that she loved Peter enough to continue to wait. But hearing about her new friend's endless Super Hero encounters was making it hard.

An excited young man ran past the line. "Spider-Man and Venom are fighting in the food court!" he yelled. "Pizza is flying everywhere!"

Candy Cane Man grabbed his camera phone. "Can you hold my place in line?" he asked Aunt May. He ran toward the food court without waiting for an answer.

Aunt May had found her companion's stories a bit boring, but that had nothing to do with the Super Heroes he mentioned. Aunt May loved Super Heroes. Especially Spider-Man. Seeing him in action did sound rather exciting.

But I promised Peter I would stay in line, Aunt May thought. Except for Candy Cane Man, no one else in the line outside Easy Ernie's was leaving. She began to wonder about Peter. She took out her cell phone and dialed her nephew's number. The call went to voicemail. She hoped Peter wasn't anywhere near the food court. She hoped he wasn't somehow caught up in the fight!

Aunt May had no idea that her nephew was, in fact, Spider-Man. As far as she knew, Peter was neither the strongest nor the quickest kid. She began to worry.

"Maybe I should go look for him," she said to herself. She was about to step out of the line when a not-so-itsy-bitsy spider came flying through the air. She landed beside the older woman.

"Everything okay here, ma'am?" Spider-Gwen asked. She knew May was Peter's aunt, but Aunt May had no idea this Spider-Woman was her nephew's friend Gwen.

"Apparently Spider-Man is battling Venom in the food court," Aunt May said. "But I cannot find my nephew,

and I'm worried he could be there."

"You stay put," Spider-Gwen said. "I'll help Spidey and make sure your nephew is safe."

"Oh, thank you," said Aunt May.

"That's what I'm here for," Spider-Gwen replied. She shot a web toward the ceiling and swung out of sight.

Chapter 7

Crash!

Spider-Man landed on a mountain of crushed presents. Confetti snow surrounded him. Giant candy canes lined the walls. A large, decorated Christmas tree stood beside an oversize green chair. Milk and cookies sat on the table next to it.

"Sweet Christmas," Spider-Man said. He rubbed his jaw where Venom had landed the punch that sent him flying from the food court into Santa's village.

"Need a hand?" two elves named Bridget and Winston asked in unison. Together they held out a giant candy cane. Spider-Man took one end. They pulled.

"Thanks," Spider-Man said when he was back on his feet. "That punch nearly knocked my stockings off."

"Thank you for defending us, Spidey," Winston said. "You're the best, if we do say so our-*elves*!"

"It's *snow* big deal," Spider-Man replied. He gestured to the empty chair by the milk and cookies. "Before I get back to my seasonal shenanigans, I have to ask. Where's the big guy? I was kind of hoping we could chat."

"Quick trip to the North Pole,"

idget said. "If there's a special present you want, we'd be happy to tell him."

Before Spider-Man could say Stark Smart Watch, Venom burst in.

"Oh, he is definitely on the naughty list," said Winston.

"Spider-Man, catch!" Bridget hollered. She tossed a giant candy cane to the web-slinger. He caught it and thrust it at Venom.

The alien grabbed the swinging sweet and snapped it in two. "Silly spider," it hissed. "Your sugary spear is no match for us!"

Venom began to separate from its host. The black goo reached for Spider-Man. "Join us and we will have more strength. We will have more power. We will have more everything!"

Spider-Man did a backflip onto Santa's chair. "More, more, more. We, we, we. Is that all you ever think of?" He spun a web-wall, creating a barrier between the sticky liquid and himself. Venom's oozing black tendrils caught in the web. "Thanks for the offer," Spider-Man said. "But I prefer my friends less squishy. More solid."

The alien goo untangled itself from the web. It reattached to its host.

"If you will not have us, then we will destroy you!" Venom hissed.

"Now you're feeling the festive spirit," Spidey said. "I can't wait to read your holiday card."

Spider-Man shot his webs at Venom.

The alien caught them and pulled.

Spider-Man sailed through the air like a stone from a slingshot.

He flew out the door of Santa's workshop. He crash-landed on a pile of

golden gelt in the middle of a Hanukkah display. An oversize dreidel spun off its perch and landed on top of him.

Spider-Gwen stood above him. "Ouch," she said. "Your head must be spinning!"

Chapter 8

"Boy, am I glad to see you," Spider-Man said. He was stuck between the dreidel and the Hanukkah gelt. He held out his arm for a tug.

Spider-Gwen did not move.

"In case you missed it," Spidey added, "Venom is here and he's a bit of a handful. I could really use some help."

Spider-Gwen crossed her arms. "So now *you* need *my* help?" she asked.

Spider-Man hung his head.

"What about when I needed *your* help?" she continued. "I ended up with a book for my dad about a running exercise called a fartlek!" She tossed the heavy book to Spidey. He caught it with his free hand.

"Heh, heh," Spider-Man laughed. "It has the word *fart* in it."

"I know it was a bad choice!" Gwen said. "That's why I needed your help. And you weren't there for me."

Spider-Man stopped laughing. He realized his selfish behavior was a lot like Venom's. More, more, more. Me, me, me. "You're right," he said. "I'm sorry. I should have helped you. All I've thought about today is myself." He sighed. "I even left Aunt May to wait in a really long line, just for a present for me. I knew she had other things to do. But all that stops now. As soon as we take down Venom, I will make it up to you. I will stop being the spoiled, big-headed, annoying—"

"Fartlek!" Spider-Gwen cried.

"Um, what?"

"Toss me the fartlek!"

A hiss echoed behind Spider-Man. He threw the book to Spider-Gwen. She caught it and hurled it straight at Venom's chest. The villain flew backward just before it could grab Spidey.

Spider-Gwen shoved the large dreidel off of Spider-Man, freeing her friend. Then she charged at Venom.

The alien got to its feet. It swiped at Spider-Gwen. She ducked. She kicked at it. Venom jumped out of the way.

"You are not the spider we want," Venom hissed. "But you will do."

Its gooey tendrils reached for Spider-Gwen.

"Gee, thanks," she said as she ran away. "You really know how to sweet-talk a girl."

She scaled the walls. Venom followed. She jumped between beams. The alien did the same. Venom was fast. It was gaining on her. It was only a matter of seconds before Venom would catch Spider-Gwen!

Suddenly, a drone decorated in gold jingling bells zoomed between the hero and her pursuer. Venom clutched its ears to block out the painful sound. It fell to the ground.

Spider-Gwen was safe for now.

She swung over to the toy store where Spider-Man was standing. He held a remote control. He twisted a knob and the jingling drone flew to his side.

"This is so going on my wish list," he said.

Spider-Gwen shook her head.

"Sorry," said Spidey. "Not about me right now."

Spider-Gwen took the drone and gave the bells a shake. "But it might just be about these." She turned to Spider-Man. "Keep the big guy distracted for a minute, then meet me by the carolers. I have an idea."

Chapter 9

"And that's where you come in," Spider-Gwen said. She was standing in front of a music store, addressing a group of carolers. She had just explained that Spider-Man and Venom would be arriving any moment and that she needed the carolers' help.

The carolers were speechless. Fighting bad guys was not part of their holiday playlist. The youngest caroler was a girl named Grace. Normally, Grace was shy. But she was also brave. Grace could speak up when something was important. And being asked to help defeat a Super Villain felt very important. Grace raised her hand.

"Yes?" Spider-Gwen asked.

"You're a Super Hero," Grace said. "What can we do that you can't?"

Spider-Gwen leaned forward until she was face-to-face with Grace. "You can sing, right?"

The girl nodded.

Spider-Gwen tossed her a handbell. "Then let's try 'Jingle Bells' on four."

Less than a minute later, Spider-Man came swinging down the mall's hall. Venom was right behind him.

"I really hope Gwen's plan works," Spidey said to himself. "Because if she's wrong, I might be in for an alien abduction!"

Spider-Gwen caught sight of Spidey. She jumped behind a drum kit that she'd borrowed from the music store. The carolers stood around her, each holding a chime or bell. Spider-Gwen grabbed a pair of drumsticks. She tapped them together and counted, "One, two, three, four!"

Thus began a truly rocking version of "Jingle Bells."

The sound reached Venom. The alien began to screech. It tried to escape, but Spider-Man stopped it with a well-timed jab.

Spider-Gwen pounded on the drums. The carolers rang their bells. Venom started to separate from its host. Grace sang louder!

Finally, the black alien goo detached completely from the human it had controlled. Without a body to give it shape, the creature became a wad of sticky gunk. It looked harmless, but it was still dangerous. It needed to be contained.

Spider-Man ran over to a holiday shopper. "Would you mind?" he asked, pointing to an unused present box and some ribbon. The shopper handed the items over right away.

Spidey wrestled the venomous glop into the box. He slammed the lid shut. The box rattled. It shook. The creature was still trying to fight its way out. Spider-Man sat on the lid and reached for the tape. Then he wrapped a ribbon around the box and tied a bow. Nice and tight.

Chapter 10

Spider-Man, Spider-Gwen, and the gift box that contained Venom sat on a bench listening to the carolers sing. The Super Heroes were discussing what to do with the box when two police officers arrived.

"Aw, Spider-Man. You shouldn't have," said Officer Ditko. He grinned as he reached for the present.

"You might not want to open that, Officer," Spider-Gwen said. "It has an alien parasite inside that will take over your body and make you a Super Villain."

Officer Ditko sighed. "Of course it does."

His partner, Officer Stanley, carefully lifted the box. "I guess we can't leave it here," she said. "Any ideas about what we should do with it?"

"Give it to Tony Stark," Spider-Man suggested. "But tell Iron Man no returns!"

"Will do," said Officer Stanley. "Thanks, Spider-friends. And happy holidays."

As the police officers walked away, Spider-Man turned to Spider-Gwen. "I'm sorry again that I didn't help when you asked me to today. I would like to help you find the perfect present for your father. If you'll let me."

"Thanks," said Spider-Gwen. "That would be great."

"I'll meet you in the bookstore in an hour," Spidey said. "There's something I have to take care of first."

Spider-Man raised his web-shooters. He spun a web into the air. He swung out of sight.

Chapter
11

"That's when she went bananas on the drums," Candy Cane Man said. The gentleman who had asked Aunt May to hold his place in line so he could witness the Super Hero battle was back at Easy Ernie's. He showed Aunt May pictures of Spider-Man and Spider-Gwen on his camera phone.

"I didn't know she was a drummer. How did she sound?" Aunt May asked.

"Fantastic!" he replied. "Maybe that's one of her super powers."

"Exciting," said Aunt May. She was

scrolling through more photographs when someone nearby cleared his throat.

"Hi, Aunt May," Peter said. May looked up to see her nephew standing beside her. He held a wrapped present in his hand.

"There you are!" she said. "Peter, I am so relieved you are all right. Did

you hear that Spider-Man was at the mall? He and his lovely Spider-Woman friend saved us from an angry alien. My fellow line-stander here took some wonderful photographs of the event. Would you like to see them?"

"No, thank you," Peter said. "Though I'm sure they're terrific."

"I only take pictures of life's best moments," Candy Cane Man replied with a huff.

"It's just that we can't stay any longer," Peter said. "Aunt May, can I take you to lunch?"

Aunt May looked down the line. Though it had moved slightly, there were still at least twenty people ahead of her. "But, Peter," she said. "If we go to lunch now, we will lose our place in line. You won't get your Stark Smart Watch. I don't want you to miss out on the present that could change your life."

Peter shrugged. "My life is pretty great already," he said. "The only thing that could make it better is being with someone I love. I'm sorry I was too self-centered to see that."

Peter held the gift out to Aunt May. "And the only present I need is this one to give to you."

Aunt May smiled. She took the package and unwrapped it. "The new Agatha Twisty mystery!" she said. "Oh, thank you, Peter. I love it." Aunt May hugged her nephew and took his hand. "To be honest," she added, "I am a bit peckish. Woman cannot survive on candy canes alone." Aunt May said good-bye to her new line-friend and followed Peter away from Easy Ernie's.

"Want to go to the food court?" he asked. "I hear they've got eggnog egg rolls."

Aunt May laughed. "Sounds delicious!"

As Peter Parker and his aunt walked hand in hand toward the food court, Candy Cane Man pulled his phone from his pocket. He lifted it to take a picture. *CLICK*.

"Life's best moments," he said.